LOST AT SEA

LOST AT SEA

Jonathan Neale

Houghton Mifflin Company

Boston 2002

For information about permission to reproduce selections from this book,
write to Permissions, Houghton Mifflin Company,
215 Park Avenue South, New York, New York 10003.

www.houghtonmifflinbooks.com

Book design by Lisa Diercks
The text of this book is set in ITC Mendoza Roman Book.

Library of Congress Cataloging-in-Publication Data
Neale, Jonathan.
Lost at sea / by Jonathan Neale.
p. cm.
Summary: A brother and sister recount their harrowing experiences as
they sail a small yacht across the Atlantic Ocean, after their mentally
unstable mother's boyfriend is washed overboard.
RNF ISBN 0-618-13920-6 PAP ISBN 0-618-43236-1
[1. Survival—Fiction. 2. Sailing—Fiction. 3. Brothers and sisters—Fiction.
4. Mentally ill—Fiction.] I. Title.
PZ7.N27 Lo 2002
[Fic]—dc21   00-068251

Manufactured in the United States of America
HAD 10 9 8 7 6 5 4 3 2 1

For my mother

LOST AT SEA

One

Orrie

The week before we got lost at sea I was lying on a beach in the Canary Islands with my brother Jack. The sand was warm under our backs. The sun was roasting my tummy. We watched white clouds move fast across a blue sky.

"Mum's making another mistake," I said.

"Skip's all right," Jack said.

Skip is Mum's boyfriend. Skip is the mistake.

"He's too loud," I said.

"That's because he's nervous," Jack said.

"I know that. I'm not stupid."

Jack is twelve and he's always trying to be mature and

understanding. He still thinks the same things I do, but he won't say them any more.

Really I don't like Skip because he keeps doing this thing to me.

It's too embarrassing to talk about.

Every time he sees me he pats me on the head.

I'm eleven years old. I don't forgive.

"Mum needs some love," Jack said.

"Dad won't do?" I said. I knew it was a stupid thing to say as soon as I said it. Our parents are divorced. Jack didn't say anything.

"See that cloud that looks like a cow?" I said.

"Yes," Jack said.

I knew he didn't. The whole beach was littered with women and girls with their tops off. It was all hot and sophisticated and European. Great blobs of white women everywhere. I knew Jack wasn't looking at the clouds. The way I could tell was every time I looked over at him he was carefully looking up at the sky.

Up till this year I didn't wear my top at the beach, either. Now of course I do. Mum and me had a sort of argument about it the first day at the beach.

She asked me why I didn't take my top off.

I told her she'd still be taking her top off when she was fifty. She won't care if people look at her and throw up behind her back. I didn't say that last bit.

She said in her sweet voice, the one the social workers use before they send you to the gas chamber, "Orrie, most girls don't have breasts when they're eleven. You shouldn't worry about it. Lots of girls don't develop until they're fourteen or fifteen."

The whole beach was listening.

Anyway, "See that girl over there?" I said to Jack.

"No."

He knew who I meant all right. She was about twenty feet away. She looked about thirteen. And she looked like she'd had breasts at eleven.

"The blond one," I said.

"No," Jack said, looking straight up at the sky.

"The one with just the little orange bottoms on."

Jack's whole body turned red with embarrassment. Winding my brother up is like shooting babies after you nail their feet to the floor.

"I'm going to go over and tell her you fancy her," I said.

"Please don't," Jack whispered.

I wouldn't really do it. I love my brother. Anybody messes with my brother, I'll tear their face off and feed it to the toilet.

I went over to the blond girl. She was making sandcastles like a little kid. So I sat down and helped her. I get on well with people. She was German and her name was Ilse.

After about ten minutes Jack came over. He sort of stood there not knowing what to do.

I introduced them. I said, "Ilse, this is my Little Baby Brother, Mudcake."

The devil made me do it.

We're supposed to be in the Canary Islands for two weeks' holiday. Skip has this boat and he's sailing it down from Gibraltar to meet us. Jack thinks it's pretty special Skip has a boat. Mum and Skip have been going out about six months. It looks like they're getting serious.

I have another brother. His name's Andy and he's seven. He woke me up really early the next morning. It was still dark.

"Orrie," he said quietly.

I turned on the light. He was standing by the bed. He's a very cute kid, all freckles and blond hair. I keep telling Mum we should sell him for TV ads and use the money to buy a castle in Scotland.

"What is it?" I said. I'm not at my best in the early morning.

"Promise you won't tell," Andy said.

"Promise." I put on my bathing suit and my blue sweater with the penguin on it and followed Andy down to the beach.

Andy was carrying some leftover fish from dinner at the restaurant the night before—the head and bones and stuff. I'm a vegetarian. The whole rest of my family aren't. They can eat whatever they want to eat. They'll pay for it in their future lives.

Andy took me down to the rock breakwater that sticks out into the bay. He sat by the edge of the sea and dropped the leftover bits of fish on a rock just under the water.

First one crab came out from under the rock. Then another and another. They all started feeding on the fish, pushing at each other and snapping their blue and red claws.

"It's the crab family," Andy said. He sounded really proud. He pointed at the biggest crab. "That's the daddy." He pointed at the smallest crab. "That's the baby."

"What's the baby's name?"

"Andy," Andy said.

"Is this the secret?"

"Yes," he said.

But I knew it wasn't the secret.

We sat on the breakwater and watched the sun come up.

"We're going to go round the world," Andy said.

"No, we're not," I said. I didn't tell him not to make things up. Little kids make things up in their heads all day long.

"We're going to go round the world on Skip's boat," Andy said.

"How do you know?" I said.

"I heard Mum and Skip talking on the phone," Andy said. The bottom dropped out of my world.

Some people would be excited to go round the world.

They don't know my mother. My mother has dreams and they go wrong.

"You scared?" I asked Andy.

My little brother nodded.

"Don't be," I said. "Everything's going to be all right."

I'm turning into a grownup. As soon as things start to go wrong, I start lying to the children.

My Mum looks at things. The first time Andy walked to the supermarket took forever. He was one back then and just learning to walk. I can do it in six minutes, but I'm fast. Andy and Mum stopped to look at house after house. Mum would say look at the windows. We looked. "Pretty," Andy said. We looked at the garbage in people's yards. "These people use green garbage bags," Mum would say. Andy would nod.

They kept squatting down to look at the cracks in the pavement. They got me doing it. We would just sit there and stare at the cracks. They got very complicated if you looked at them long enough.

"Imagine you were small enough to live in the crack," Mum said.

We did, for a while.

"Nobody step on me," Andy said.

"Hide under the cliffs," Mum said.

It was a good way to learn to walk to the supermarket.

My mum has a crack in her personality now and we all have to help her.

When we got back to the hotel Mum told us Skip had sailed in and we were all having dinner on the boat tonight.

"I don't want to go on his boat," I said. We were only supposed to be on a two-week holiday. My dad's parents paid for it. My mum doesn't have any money. She's English. My dad's parents are American. We live in England. I'm both— English and American.

"Orrie," Mum said, and she looked at me with big wet sad eyes. My name's Orchid. Everybody calls me Orrie. My brother Jack's real name is Sky. Everybody calls him Jack. But the time Andy was born my parents were normal, so they gave him a real name.

Nobody knows me here. I'm going to make them call me Fran.

Mum and Andy looked at pebbles next to the breakwater. They sat there for two hours, picking up one pebble after another. Every once in a while Andy said "Color" or "Spot." Mum said "Mmm." I got bored sunbathing so I went and sat by them. Andy handed me each pebble after he'd spent forever looking at it, turning it over. Then I looked at it.

Every pebble in the world is different.

Skip's boat is called *Good Company*. It's not like the other yachts in the harbor. They're all long and sleek and painted bright white. *Good Company* is red and small and sort of round and stubby, with short masts and ropes and buckets all over the deck. It looks like somebody lives in it.

Skip put out a hand to help me aboard. I ignored it. I know how to jump onto boats.

I jumped from the dock, no problem. Skip patted me on the head. "Welcome aboard, Orrie," he said.

"My name's Fran," I said.

Skip tried hard. He had this little tiny kitchen down below, with four beds in it and a table and a little stove with two burners. He made me a special separate veggie dish. It was pasta. It's always pasta when they make you a special separate veggie dish. But it tasted OK.

Skip and Mum sat on a bunk on one side of the table and us kids sat on a bunk on the other side. Skip put his arm round Mum and leaned back.

"Children," Mum said, "Skip and I have an announcement to make."

Skip smiled at us.

"We're all going to sail across the Atlantic together on *Good Company*." She looked at us, all expecting.

Jack's face lit up like Christmas. He loves boats. "When do we leave?"

"The day after tomorrow," Mum said.

I threw my pasta at her and jumped off the bunk and ran up the little ladder and out onto the deck.

Jack

My sister Orrie threw her bowl of pasta in Mum's face and it fell off onto her lap. The spaghetti sauce ran down Mum's face, all red and lumpy. Mum just sort of sat there flapping her hands. She doesn't know how to deal with Orrie. She looked at Skip for help. He didn't know what to do, either. He just sort of looked embarrassed. I was pretty embarrassed by my family too.

My little brother Andy said, "Can I take my crabs?" I don't know what that was about. Andy lives in a world of his own. Nobody paid him any attention.

I didn't say anything. I just got up carefully and went on deck. I fix things in my family. I don't like doing it. Somebody else ought to fix things. But I'm old enough to do it, so I do it.

Orrie was sitting on the bowsprit. That's the round piece of wood that sticks out from the front of the boat. She was holding onto the jib stay, the wire rope you clip the front sail onto. Her feet dangled over the water.

I sat down next to her. I didn't say anything. Sometimes it's best to be quiet with Orrie. We're brother and sister.

There were stars in the sky, and the lights of houses went

up the black hill from the harbor. I could hear the water lapping against *Good Company*'s hull.

"We're never going to see Dad again," Orrie said.

"Of course we are," I said.

"You just want to sail across the Atlantic," Orrie said.

I took my time thinking that one over. "That's true," I said.

"You don't care about Dad," she said.

You can see why she gets into fights.

I didn't say anything. We just sat there some more in the dark until Orrie started crying. I put my arm around her, remembering to hold onto the jib stay with my other hand so we wouldn't fall in.

Orrie

Jack and Mum wanted to go. I didn't. Nobody paid any attention to what I wanted, of course. But I made them let me call Dad first. They weren't going to let me, but I said if they didn't I'd phone anyway. They knew I meant it because I've done it before. I call up Dad collect and he always takes the call. Mum doesn't have any money.

I called at eight in the morning, so it was three in the morning in New York where Dad was. He didn't say anything about that. He wants me to be able to call anytime.

I told him what was happening. He said to put Mum on.

They had a big fight. I could tell Dad was pissed at Mum for ruining all our lives. Mum was crying and saying, "Why do you always do this?" in that whiny voice that makes you want to push a pie in her face.

Andy went and hid under the bed like he usually does. And let me tell you, I wanted to hide under that bed too.

"That's not fair," Mum screamed at the phone. Then she handed the phone to Jack and said, "Here. You talk to your father."

"Hi," Jack said. He always sounds more American when he talks to Dad.

Then Jack betrayed us. He told Dad *Good Company* looked seaworthy. He said Skip had sailed all over the Mediterranean and the Indian Ocean. He said he and Andy were really looking forward to the voyage.

"Andy's hiding under the bed," I shouted loud enough for Dad to hear.

Jack explained to Dad that Andy was hiding under the bed because Mum and Dad had been fighting. He said it to make Dad feel guilty. Dad already feels so guilty for leaving all of us because Mum's a tootie frootie.

"Here," Jack said, and he handed me the phone.

Dad told me he'd talk to Skip and if it sounded like everything was all right we could go. He said it sounded like the chance of a lifetime for me and Jack.

He meant it would be an adventure for Jack, because he's a boy.

Dad asked me not to upset Mum too much. And he said he'd fly down to Antigua, the island in the West Indies we're going to. As we come sailing into the harbor, he'll be standing there on the dock with his arms open wide. "Your mother needs to make a new life for herself, Chuckle Bunny," Dad said. "Let me talk to her now."

"Promise you'll meet us in Antigua, Dad?"

"Promise."

I passed Mum the phone. If my Dad told me to cut my feet off and put them in the fridge for breakfast, I'd do it. I was in the bathroom when God passed out the brains.

Two

Jack

I came across Orrie's friend Ilse on the beach. She was making sandcastles again. "Hullo, Mudcake," she said.

I shrugged my shoulders and tried to look cool.

"Help me," she said. We made a humongous castle. I told her about when we were little and there were rainy days Mum used to let us play with blankets. We would get all the blankets and sheets and pillows off all the beds and furniture in the house and make a big pile in the middle of the living room. Then Mum played with us inside the pile. Sometimes we were dwarves looking for gold. Sometimes it was my gold and I was the dragon. Sometimes we were moles trying to drag chocolate bars back through little tunnels to feed our hungry children. At bedtime each of us would just gather up whatever blankets or sheets or whatever we wanted and carry it off to our beds. That's why we kept getting the bedclothes changed around when it rained.

"Your mother is not very rules," Ilse said. I love the way she speaks English.

"No," I said.

"Good," Ilse said.

Orrie

My German friend Ilse came down to see us off across the Atlantic. Jack was standing on the front of the boat, holding on to some rope thing. When he saw Ilse he took his T-shirt off so she could see his muscles. He thinks he has chest muscles. I know this. He looks at them in the mirror.

He waved his T-shirt to Ilse as we set off to sea. He doesn't know how obvious he is.

Jack

Ilse came down to see me off. There were a few fluffy white clouds high in the sky. The boat leapt to meet the water. Orrie was sick almost immediately.

I told her: "I told you to take the seasick pills."

She muttered something.

She was lying on the deck with her face over the side of

the boat. But she had her safety harness clipped onto one of the long safety ropes that go right round the boat. The harness is made out of rope and goes round your shoulder and waist. Skip says you're supposed to wear it and stay clipped on all the time you're on deck. That way you stay tied to the boat no matter how much it rolls.

It was rolling.

"You want me to get you some pills?" I said.

"I don't take pills," Orrie said.

I went and got the pills.

I can't explain everything about the boat, but I've drawn a couple of pictures I hope make sense.

There are two short masts: the mainmast with the mainsail and the mizzenmast with the mizzen sail. The sail clips on in front.

The wheelhouse is the thing in the middle of the boat that looks like a garden shed on top of the deck. It keeps

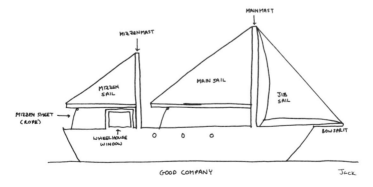

GOOD COMPANY   Jack

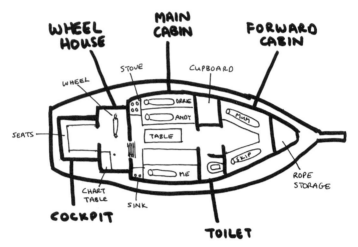

WHEEL HOUSE   MAIN CABIN   FORWARD CABIN

STOVE   CUPBOARD

WHEEL

ORRIE

ANDY

MUM

TABLE

SEATS

SKIP

ME

ROPE STORAGE

CHART TABLE

SINK

COCKPIT

TOILET

GOOD COMPANY LOOKING DOWN AS IF DECK WAS CUT OFF

Jack

you dry when you're at the wheel steering the boat. There are big glass windows all round the wheelhouse so you can see out in every direction and don't run into anything.

Orrie said she didn't want to take the pills. So I held her mouth open like she was a sick dog and shoved the pills in.

She threw up on my hand. Some people have no sense.

The surprising thing is how small the boat is. Five people on top of each other, and you're never more than twelve feet from somebody. Ever. You really have to get on. Mum and Skip have the little forward cabin with the two bunks to themselves. I suppose that's all right, not that it's any of my business.

Me and Andy and Orrie sleep in the main cabin, which

has four bunks and a table and a small cooker. There's a little ladder up to the wheelhouse. Skip is teaching me to steer.

When it got dark I went out on deck to get Orrie. She was lying there in the dark with her head over the side.

"Time to go below, Orrie," I said.

"Leave me here to die," she said. "It's kinder in the long run."

I was glad she was able to make jokes. But as I unclipped her safety harness I held onto the rope myself in case she stumbled or there was a freak wave as I was getting her below.

Orrie

Jack pushed me into my bunk. I have one of the outside bunks in the main cabin. I just lay in my sleeping bag with the little curtain pulled so nobody has to look at me. It's like a coffin. There's maybe a foot above my face. The outside wall of my bunk is the outside wall of the boat. The other side is under water. The sea is about a foot from my ear.

The thing they don't tell you about the ocean is how big the waves are. Bigger than the boat. The boat rides up the waves, up and up and teetering at the top, and then down, getting faster, slamming into the sea with a great bang right by my ear. Each time we hit it sounds like the water will punch a great hole in the side of the boat.

I'd already chucked up everything in my stomach, so I just lay there and dry-heaved.

I didn't sleep. In the middle of the night I got up and went up the ladder to the wheelhouse. Skip was standing in a dim light, one hand on the wheel and the other holding onto the wheelhouse ceiling.

"Are we going to die?" I asked him.

"No," Skip said.

"In the storm," I said. "Are we going to die in the storm?"

"There is no storm, Fran."

I didn't want him to laugh at me then.

He didn't. He said it was a normal night with a gentle breeze. Skip said everybody got seasick. He told me to go lie down under the little kitchen table in the middle of the main cabin. Skip said it was the most middle place in the whole boat. It's in the middle of the front and back. It's in the middle from top to bottom. And it's in the middle from side to side. So no matter which way the boat rocks and rolls, you stay pretty still because you're in the middle.

I tried it. It's colder under the table, but it's better. And it's quieter, so I wasn't so scared by the noise of the sea. I got some sleep.

Jack stepped on me when he got up to take his turn at the wheel.

Jack

Orrie yelled at me when I got up. Skip turned the wheel over to me and went below. I could tell he only went and lay in my bunk, he didn't go forward where Mum was. I'm pretty sure he didn't go to sleep. He was showing me he trusted me to steer at night, but sort of making sure he was awake, too, in case anything went wrong. I liked that.

After about an hour Skip popped his head up the ladder and asked quietly if everything was all right.

I said yes. I asked him what to do if I was alone at night and had to pee.

"You could go below," Skip said. "But the old boat would be yawing pretty quick, and you'd probably have to run back up with your pants around your ankles. Best thing is to pop out fast and hang onto the wire stays and pee over the side."

I nodded.

"Always pee over the side away from the wind. Or it blows right back on you."

I nodded.

"Don't forget your harness," Skip said, and he took the wheel from me.

I put on my safety harness and went outside and clipped the harness to the safety rope. Then I stood on the rail on the edge of the boat and held one wire stay in each hand, with my arms outstretched. The boat rose and fell. The black water seemed to come up at me and then fall away. The sky was full of stars. My willie got cold but my heart sang.

I went back into the wheelhouse and Skip went out for a

pee. I noticed he didn't take a harness. I didn't say anything. Skip knows what he's doing.

Orrie

I felt a bit better this morning.

"Hey," Skip shouted happily. He was holding the top of some cooking pot. "Look! Crabs. Great."

Just the thought of somebody eating crabs made me not better any longer.

"With butter," Skip said. "I love crabs with butter and mayonnaise."

The crabs were alive. I could hear them scuttling and clanking against the side of the pot. My skin crawled.

"Mum," Andy screamed. "Skip's going to eat my crab family."

Jack

Today Skip showed me everything while Orrie sunbathed and Mum steered the boat. Skip came up behind Mum and kissed her on the back of the neck, which I thought showed style. You could see it made her feel good.

Maybe in Antigua I'll meet another German tourist like Ilse and just sort of calmly go up behind her and kiss her on the back of the neck and see what happens. After I get to know her, of course, or she'll probably hit me.

Skip showed me how to "shoot the sun" with a sextant

to find the angle of the sun, and how to look at the map and do all the math afterward to find out exactly where you are. I couldn't do all the numbers, but I more or less followed. I'm pretty good at math in school. Only Charles Cresswell is better, and he's from the planet Trafalmadore.

Skip explained that lots of yuppies have satellite navigation systems, but they cost thousands of bucks. The sextant costs fifty, works just fine, and has been around for hundreds of years.

Skip likes the old ways.

He showed me the bucket of rope in the cockpit in the stern. One end of the rope is tied to the boat. If somebody falls overboard you just throw the bucket over the side and the rope unwinds behind you.

"It's fast," Skip said, "and it won't kink. Looks messy, but it works a lot better than all those fancy coils of rope you see on the yachts."

I think he's good for Mum.

"Do you have a real name?" I asked Skip. We were sitting in the cockpit looking out at the sea while Mum took another turn steering.

"What do you mean?" Skip said.

"Like everybody calls me Jack, but it's not my real name."

"What's your real name?" he said.

I wanted Skip to be my friend, so I told him. He laughed at me, a big belly laugh.

I looked at the sea. Skip turned sideways and stared at my face. "I'm sorry," Skip said.

"It's OK," I said. "Everyone laughs at my name." It wasn't OK.

"My real name's Ignatius," Skip said.

He waited. I turned my face away from him so he wouldn't see it and pretended I was looking out to sea.

After a while he said, "Thanks for not laughing."

"Ignatius is OK," I said.

"When I was Andy's age other boys used to call me Iggy and poke me with sticks," Skip said.

"That's horrible," I said. I wanted to know if the sticks were pointed, but I didn't ask.

"I'm called Skip now because I have this boat. Skip is short for Skipper, which means captain."

"Thanks for telling me about the Ignatius thing," I said.

"You could be called Skip too when you grow up."

"I'd like that," I said.

"All you have to do is buy a boat," he said.

Orrie

Sunbathing healed me. Mum made me some thin soup. I ate a bit to keep her happy.

Skip showed me how to steer. He let me take the wheel

by myself for thirty minutes while he just sat over in the corner of the wheelhouse. He didn't keep saying things the way most people do when you're trying to learn something. He let me get on with it.

Afterward Skip said I did good, but I can't stand a watch at night yet and take the wheel by myself when everybody's asleep, like Jack does. Skip said it's because I've been sick, and we have to wait for my stomach to settle.

In reality, of course, he's sexist.

Jack

Maybe Orrie is right about Skip. He's a bit crazy. He stopped to do something at the foot of the ladder before he came up to take over the wheel at three in the morning. It only took him a few minutes, but I was dog tired. I'd been wrestling with the wheel for three hours. It was hell to hold it.

"What were you doing?" I asked when he came up.

He had a can in his hand. He looked at the can. "Just between you and me?"

I nodded. I was too tired to talk much.

"Man to man?" he said. "Keep a secret?"

"Yes."

"You know the engine?"

I nodded. The engine's underneath the wheelhouse. We get to it by taking up some floorboards behind the main cabin. We use it to get in and out of harbor.

"It's a Perkins," Skip said. "Works as well as it did twenty years ago, the day it was made. But I don't like engines. I like a sail. A man, the sea, and the wind. No machines. That's how it's meant to be. Clean. You just ride the wind and take the gifts of the sea."

He smiled at me.

"Women want you to use the engine. Maybe there isn't enough wind, you're stuck in the doldrums. Or a storm's coming. Or they got a hairdresser's appointment. They want to turn on the motor. They got somewhere to go. Hurry, hurry, hurry. Might as well be on the London tube."

"So I opened a can of Spaghetti-Os," Skip said, "and I poured it into the fuel tank."

He held up the can. I could see the Spaghetti-Os label. He's as cracked as my mother.

"No way on earth anybody can make me use that engine now," he said. "Nobody this side of a shipyard can clean that mother out now."

He took the wheel and told me to go below and get some sleep.

Orrie

I knew the moment I woke up. I started screaming.

Three

Jack

Orrie's face was about six inches from my head. She was screaming, no words. The boat was pitching and yawing, just rolling all over the place. I heard a great wave crash onto the deck.

I scrambled out of my sleeping bag and pushed past Orrie. She just stood there screaming into nothing.

"What is it?" Andy said.

"Nothing," I said, and grabbed for the ladder to the wheelhouse. Another wave crashed onto the deck. The boat jumped and it threw me half off the ladder. I banged my elbow on something hard and the pain shot through me. But I didn't have time for it.

There was nobody at the wheel. I already knew that. The door to the deck was open. Skip's safety harness was still on its peg by the door.

I knew what happened.

I screamed his name.

The wheel was spinning on its own. Through the wheelhouse window on the side I could see a great shadow, a wall of water rising above us in the darkness. The boat was rolling between the waves. It could roll over at any moment.

I screamed down at Orrie to come up and take the wheel and plunged out the wheelhouse door. I grabbed the bucket of rope and threw it overboard. It uncoiled like it had been shot from a gun. I realized I had forgotten my safety harness.

Orrie

Jack yelled something, God knows what, from upstairs. Andy was whimpering and gulping and the boat was rolling. I had to brace myself against the table to stand up. Mum came out of the little forward cabin, wearing a nightgown.

A long white nightgown. Her hair was dark against the white. Her face was all scrunched.

"What happened?" Mum said, and I didn't tell her.

The boat sort of fell over on its side. Oh God, I thought, God, God, God, please—and I don't even believe in God.

We waited, the boat halfway over, on its side. Mum was

thrown on her back, lying down against what had been the wall. "Oh God," I said, "God, God, God."

"Mum," Andy wailed.

Jack

The boat tipped over on its side and threw me across the cockpit. I grabbed the wire stays and held on with both hands as I went over the side and under the water.

It was like a great weight pushing in on my chest from all sides. I didn't open my eyes. I didn't dare open anything. Don't let the water in my mouth, I thought. When I finally did open my eyes the water was black. My arms were stretched above me like I was hanging from a cliff. I couldn't pull myself up. I wasn't strong enough. I could feel the water dragging me under.

Orrie

It felt like forever. It was maybe thirty seconds. Then the boat moved and straightened itself. Mum fell back across the cabin and into my arms. I'm smaller than her. My head was about at her breasts.

"Orrie," she said, "Orrie." And then she made a little sound like a trapped animal. I didn't like it. I tried to get away, but she had hold of the back of my sweater.

I didn't know what had happened to Jack.

"Jack," I shouted.

No answer. The boat rolled again.

"Jack," I screamed. No answer.

"Mum!" I shook my body in her arms, trying to get free. Her fingers held me.

"Mum, Jack's—" and then I didn't want to say the word.

Mum wouldn't let me go even for Jack. I hated her then. She just kept making that stupid little noise.

The boat roll began again. We were all going to die. I knew it. Andy went to the ladder.

I screamed at him. He didn't listen, but he slipped on the ladder anyway. He's little.

"Andy, stop," I screamed.

He turned round.

"Don't go up," I said.

"Jack's in trouble," he said in a serious-little-kid way.

You'll die up there, I wanted to yell at him. Leave me one brother. "The crab family," I yelled. "They fell out of their pot. Find them before they get smashed to pieces."

Andy's face looked awful then. He came right down the steps and looked round the cabin wildly. He was so scared he couldn't see anything.

Mum was still moaning and her fingers still dug into my back.

"Skip," I said to her, in a real calm voice like the nurses use. "We have to go help Skip."

"Skip's all right?" she said.

The boat was rolling back up straight again.

"Skip's all right," I said.

She turned to look at the ladder and relaxed her claws and I wrenched myself free and ran for the ladder.

There was nobody in the wheelhouse. The back door was open. I went straight through it.

Nobody.

I shouted: "Jack."

"Orrie," he called back. Not loud. I looked. There were little white hands holding onto the stays on one side. The rest of him must be in the water. I ran over. There he was. His head and chest were out of the water. His face was blue. There was pain all over it.

"Hi," he said.

"Hi," I said, and almost laughed. I lay down along the side of the boat and reached down and grabbed his right arm. I waited for the boat to roll down toward him. Then I tried to pull him up.

I wasn't strong enough.

Jack

Orrie was lying there above me, crying.

My muscles weren't good enough.

We were leaving Skip behind, in the dark, every second

the boat sailed on. Maybe he'd grabbed the rope. Maybe we were towing him.

The sea felt so heavy, dragging me down. I didn't know how much longer I could hold on. My fingers had no feeling any more.

Orrie wasn't wearing her safety harness.

"Harness," I said. I wanted to shout, but it didn't come out a shout.

"What?" Orrie stood up, the worst possible thing, because she couldn't keep her balance.

"Harness," I said.

She looked down at me in the water. She kneeled and peered down at me. She had one hand on the stay. "You want your harness?" she said.

I made the words come out: "You haven't got your safety harness on. You'll fall in."

"Oh." She turned to go back into the wheelhouse.

Orrie

Mum was standing on deck outside the wheelhouse door. "Where's Skip?" she said.

"Mum," I said, trying to be calm, really calm. "Jack's fallen overboard. He's just hanging on by his fingers. See his fingers there?"

Mum looked. "Jack?" she said, as she careened over to the

side of the boat. Her face looked like they'd put her on drugs again or something. The boat was still rolling.

Mum kneeled down and looked over the edge at Jack.

She hadn't put a harness on either.

"Mum," I screamed. "Get a harness."

She turned to look at me. "Jack's not all right," she said, like some old lady who'd lost her mind.

"I found the Daddy," Andy said. He was standing in the wheelhouse door. He held out a crab to me.

Andy didn't have a safety harness on either. I slammed into him and carried us both back into the wheelhouse. I grabbed a safety harness and shoved it at him, shouting, "Get this on."

"I can't," Andy said. He turned the harness upside down and looked at it. "I don't know how." He was just a little kid. He was still holding the crab in his other hand.

"Stay in here or I'll kill you," I screamed at him. I grabbed two harnesses off the pegs and put one over me, getting it all tangled in my hair, swearing and screaming.

"Is Jack dead?" Andy said.

"No." I was out the door and skidded over to Mum. I snapped the rope of my harness onto the safety line and threw a harness over her.

"Jack's in the water," she said.

"Yes, Mum, I know."

"Skip's in the water too, isn't he?" Mum said.

"Yes, Mum." I didn't care about her feelings any more.

"I'm bad," Mum said. She said it like a Martian or a computer voice or something. No feelings.

"Mum. We have to get Jack out."

"Orrie," Jack said. "Take the wheel. Turn us round before the wind. Then we're safe."

I couldn't do that. I couldn't leave Jack. "Mum," I said. "We have to get him out or he'll die."

She turned to look right at me. Her face was close. Her eyes were big. She looked like she was trying to remember who I was.

"Orrie, the wheel," Jack said.

"Mum," I said. "You're bigger than me. And stronger. You have to help us. You have to help me pull Jack up."

"Oh," she said. "Of course." And she leaned down and took one arm and I took the other and we pulled.

Jack

Mum and Orrie got me onboard. I lay in the bottom of the cockpit, shivering, whooping for air. I was only thinking one thing: Skip.

Orrie

I didn't like the look of Jack. People die of cold in the ocean.

32

The sky was still dark, with a sort of dark blue behind us where the sun would come up.

"Where's Skip?" Mum said.

"Pull in the rope," Jack said.

"The rope," Mum said.

"Over the stern," Jack said. "I threw a rope."

"Get back inside the wheelhouse," I screamed at Andy. He did.

"Rope?" Mum said. She was leaning down, looking at Jack like a policewoman.

"Over the stern," Jack said. Then the shivering took him.

Mum saw the rope tied to a cleat on the stern. She lunged and grabbed it. She looked back at me, her eyes wild with hope. "Skip's on the rope," she said.

Jack was still shivering. "Steer," he said.

Mum said, "Skip's on the rope. I'm not bad."

Mum's brain was dangling by threads. She was pulling in the rope, hand over hand. It looked like hard work.

"Help me, Orrie," Mum said. "It's heavy. Skip's dragging."

I thought: there's an awful lot of drag on a long rope anyway.

"Steer," Jack said. "Straighten out. So we don't go over."

"He's dragging," Mum said. "Help me."

I went to help Mum.

The rope was heavy. It took two of us, hand over hand.

33

Mum counted the rhythm. One, two, three, pull, one, two, three, pull. Slowly the rope came in. It was so heavy I knew Mum was right. There was something on it.

Jack

Somebody had to steer. Orrie was helping Mum. Somebody had to get us straight before the wind. The sails were flapping and cracking like mad. They were going to split. We couldn't get back to find Skip if we didn't get straight.

I hauled myself up. Everything hurt. I went into the wheelhouse and threw myself across the deck at the wheel. I grabbed the spokes and made myself stand up straight. I tore at the wheel, trying to straighten the boat. I passed out.

Orrie

Mum and I were reaching the end of the rope. I saw it coming. I knew.

It was a gray tangle in the dawn light. There was no sun yet, but more light.

Mum gave a little moan and pulled on the rope harder. She wasn't counting any longer, just pulling, pulling, shouting, "Help, Orrie, help."

I helped. Breathing was hard. The end of the rope was caught in a tangle of torn fishing net. The net was awful heavy.

"Mum, no," I said.

"Skip," she said, "Skip," like she was begging someone. Or God. She made us both pull. We pulled the net up over the stern of the boat. I thought my arms would come out of my shoulders.

"Heave," Mum screamed, and slowly we pulled a dolphin out of the water. It was a small one, but as big as me. Sharks or something had taken bites out of it. Its head was stuck in the net. One sad dead eye looked at us. My mother lost her mind.

It's happened before. One moment—Mum. Next moment, her eyes are empty and she's out to lunch. Away with the fairies, Dad calls it. We're not supposed to say that in front of the doctors. Doctors are like teachers—easily shocked. But we all say it to each other. Mum says it too.

Only it sounds more fun than it is.

I ran inside the wheelhouse and pelted down the ladder and grabbed my boat knife off my bunk and ran back up the ladder. Jack was lying on the wheelhouse deck with two blankets over him, looking blue. Andy must have put the blankets over him. Andy was sitting next to Jack's head, his legs crossed like he learned at Mum's meditation class. He had a crab in each hand. He looked at me, worried.

"Hang loose, bro," I said.

"Hang loose, sis," Andy said, and I was out the door.

Mum was stroking the dolphin.

She was singing to it. I listened. She was singing *Silent Night*. Behind her the sky was growing blue. We rolled and were on top of a wave. I saw the sun.

I threw myself at the net and began slicing at it with my knife. Mum screamed at me. She pulled at me with her hands as I tore at the net. She slapped me, not hard, more like patting me on my arm and head. Any moment my knife could slice her. A bit of me wanted to. But I stopped.

"Mum," I shouted. I didn't know what to shout next.

"Don't hurt it," she said.

"Sit down," I said in my nurse voice. "Sit."

She sat, one hand on the dolphin's cheek.

"Don't throw yourself in," I said. "You have children. You have to live."

She turned her face away.

"Look at me." I said it calmly, like I was the grownup in charge.

She wouldn't.

"I'm going to cut the net loose," I said.

Her eyes had a little light in them then.

"He's out there somewhere," I said. "We have to get the boat under control, and then we have to sail back to look for him."

She nodded. We climbed to the top of the wave again, and the sun shone on the dolphin's skin.

If I got the dolphin overboard maybe my Mum would come back.

"We have to bury our dolphin now," I said. "He comes from the sea. He must go back to the sea. It's his home. It's where he must rest."

I think she understood. But she clutched at its head.

"Mum, pray for dolphin. Pray for dolphin so he can sleep. So he can go to Nirvana."

Mum wants to go to Nirvana.

She let go of the dolphin. She put her hands in front of her, palms together, like she was praying. I hacked at the net with my knife as fast as I could. Mum sang, quietly, "Silent night, holy night . . ."

She has a lovely voice. I got the net cut away and pulled the rope clear. I worked quickly—Mum might wander. I leaned over and grabbed the dolphin. I didn't like doing it. It smelled like the biggest dead fish you ever smelled. But I had to do it and I did it. It made a big splash. I'm never going to stop being a vegetarian.

"Let's go inside now, Mum, and I'll get the boat going right," I said.

She just sat there.

"Then we can go back and look for Skip," I said.

She looked at the sea behind us.

I leaned over and grabbed her.

I know the nurses at the hospital grab patients. They're not supposed to but I've seen them.

Mum held onto the seat at the edge of the cockpit with all her strength, and just kept looking at the sea behind us. She's stronger than me.

I stopped and let her go and breathed.

"You want to look out for Skip from here, don't you, Mum?" I said.

She didn't say anything, but I figured I was right. I was still worried she'd jump in. I could tie her up with the rope we'd hauled in, but that might encourage her to jump and join Skip, or look for him, or play with the dolphin.

Her caseworker, the nurse I liked, Arthur, said you must always speak to them like they're normal and understand everything. Even if they don't, he said. Even if it's all scrambled eggs in there, at least you're showing respect, he said. And usually they understand. Crazy people aren't stupid, he said, they're just out of their minds.

"Mum, you sit there and keep an eye out for Skip," I said. "I'm going to make the steering go right. You keep a lookout. If you see anything, shout to me."

She didn't do much, but I had to guess she'd heard.

The first time we took Mum to the hospital was the worst. Andy was really little. Dad put us all in the car. It was a blue car. I loved that car. I guess I was about six. We waited in the waiting room. Jack and I played that the Coke machine was an android come to take over the earth. Jack hid behind the swing doors and sniped at the android. Dad sort of bubbled Andy on his lap and looked upset. I was scared out of my mind. I sang Dad all the songs I knew.

Now I'm used to it. Last time in the hospital Mum's caseworker, Arthur, talked to me and everything. He asked me how I was finding the whole thing about Mum being in there.

I told him I was coping as well as could be expected in a person of my age.

"That bad, huh?" Arthur said.

"Yeah."

"We better get a bed ready for you too," Arthur said.

"I'd rather make love to a dead horse," I said.

Jack

When I woke up I was lying on the floor of the wheelhouse. Orrie was at the wheel. The boat was going fine. My whole body hurt. I was cold.

I sat up.

Andy showed me his crabs. "Nice, Andy," I said.

"Go sit with Mum," Orrie said. "She's out back keeping a lookout for Skip."

"We should double back," I said.

"We have," Orrie said. She was wrestling with the wheel just like I did, with it going this way and that. I had to admire her for getting it under control. She had trouble seeing over the wheel. She had to stick her head out to one side or the other to look out the glass windows. Orrie is really quite short. None of us are stupid enough to say so in front of her.

"I can't hold the Mummy and Daddy crabs and find the babies," Andy said.

"Put the Mummy and Daddy in the pot," Orrie said. "And then go find the babies."

"I can't hold the Mummy and the Daddy and go down the stairs," Andy said to Orrie. "Get me the pot?" he said to me.

"Go sit with Mum, Jack," Orrie said. "Now." Her voice was worried.

"Give me the Daddy to hold," I said to Andy, "and you go look for the pot."

He held out the crab and it bit me.

"Don't be mad," Andy said. "He didn't mean it." Andy was frightened.

"It's OK," I said. The crab was hanging on to my long finger. It didn't hurt much, compared to the rest of me.

I put out the other hand and grabbed the crab from behind. That's the safe way to do it.

"He's the Daddy crab," Andy told me.

Now I had the crab in one hand and the crab had my finger in its claw. I sort of tugged at the crab from behind. It didn't want to let go of my finger.

"Careful," Andy said. "Don't crush him."

"Go be with Mum!" Orrie shouted, almost screeching.

I went out the back door to sit with Mum, holding on to a crab that was holding on to me. I had my blanket wrapped around me.

Mum was sitting in the back of the cockpit, looking out to sea. I clipped on and sat down next to her. She didn't say anything because she is clinically depressed.

We both looked out to sea, scanning back and forth, back and forth, over and over again.

Andy came and got his crab.

The sea is enormous. Something like a man is very small and hard to see. Twice I thought I saw something, and I shouted at Orrie to head over there, and she did. Nothing both times.

We were sailing back the way we'd come. We were in the trade winds. For six months of the year the trade winds blow in one direction, from the Canaries to the West Indies. So now we were sailing into the wind. That meant we had to tack, because you can't go straight into the wind. You have to sail at an angle to it, and then back at another angle.

We were at it till early afternoon. We didn't get far. But we hadn't gone far when we were out of control, wallowing between the waves. I just wanted to sleep. My eyes hurt from looking so hard.

I knew Skip would have frozen to death in the water by the time the sun came up. I'm pretty sure once you freeze to death you sink.

"He's gone, Mum," I said.

She looked at me with big eyes like a cow.

"It's time to get some sleep, Mum."

I stood up and took her hand and led her below. She came quietly, no sign but the tears on her face.

Four

Orrie

I stood at the wheel, hour after hour after hour. I wanted to let Jack sleep. I stopped tacking toward where we'd come. I just turned and let the boat run for the West Indies. It was easier. I didn't care any more. I didn't have to fight the wheel so much. I had to fight it, but not so much.

Andy found all his crabs but the little baby one.

"He's hiding somewhere," I told Andy. "He's frightened. He'll come out when he's hungry."

"I'm hungry too," Andy said.

"The candy bars are up forward, under Mum's bunk," I said. I couldn't steer and cook at the same time.

"Can I have two?" Andy said.

"You can have as many as you want."

"How many?"

"Zillions. Bring me some too." Why not? The grownups are all dead or crazy.

Andy went to sleep by my feet after his fourth candy bar. I threw up after my fifth. I hope it was seasickness, not the beginning of an eating disorder.

As the boat tipped one way and another Andy slid up and down the wheelhouse deck in his sleep. Kids can sleep through anything.

When Andy woke up he sat up and said, "Is Skip in Nirvana?"

"Yes." My eyes hurt with tiredness from looking at the sea.

"What's Nirvana?" Andy said.

"It's a place Mum's friends believe in."

"Like heaven?" Andy said.

"Sort of."

"Why?" Andy said. He meant how, but kids say why.

"Heaven is where you go when you're good," I said. "Nirvana is where you go when you don't have to go anywhere ever again." That's what Mum's friend Rupert Bear told me. He's really a hippie, not a bear, and his eyes roll around in his head.

"Is Skip in heaven?" Andy asked.

"Go wake your brother up," I said. "Tell him it's his turn

to steer. And if he doesn't get up here pronto, I'm going to come down and pour bleach down his ear hole and destroy his brain."

Jack stumbled up and took the wheel. I stumbled down to my place under the kitchen table. I heard Andy saying "Want a candy bar?" to Jack, and then I was asleep.

Andy woke me up. I felt like I hadn't slept at all.

Jack was at the wheel.

"It would take us weeks to get back, tacking into the wind," Jack said.

"Start the motor," I said. "Then we won't have to tack. We can sail straight back to the Canaries in four days."

Jack didn't say anything.

"Three days," I said. "Hot baths. Cute German girls. The floor won't move." I was trying to jolly him along. It didn't work. I got serious. "Start the motor."

"I can't," Jack said in a small, angry voice. "It won't work."

"Why not?"

Jack

I couldn't tell Orrie about the Spaghetti-Os. It was the last thing Skip did. I went down to the engine.

I turned it on.

It started.

Up in the wheelhouse Orrie cheered.

I stood up and wiped the grease off my hands with a kitchen towel.

The engine died.

I started it again.

It died.

Again.

Again.

Spaghetti-Os. They'd be all over the pistons now. I should have drained the fuel first.

Orrie

Jack's head stuck up the ladder. "I'm sorry," he said.

"You turned it off on purpose," I said.

"I'm going to bed," Jack said.

He must have done it on purpose. "Fix it," I said.

"I can't. I don't know how."

"Skip showed you," I said. "What are you? A man or a boy with an eensy-weensy twiddle widdle?"

He went to fix it.

I was being sexist, but it was an emergency.

Jack

I didn't know what to do. I got a wrench and just started trying to undo some nuts on top of the engine. I didn't even know what they were. I couldn't move the nuts. They were rusted. I was too weak. They weren't supposed to move. I don't know. My hand slipped and I banged my knuckles against something hard and tore the skin.

I put my hand to my mouth and got grease all in my mouth.

I saw a little blue crab on top of the engine.

"Hey, Andy," I shouted. "I found your baby crab."

He came running.

Orrie

Jack came up about half an hour later. He was crying and using swear words. He had a dirty kitchen towel wrapped around his right hand. There were blood smears all over the towel. He said he couldn't fix the engine. He said he didn't know how. He said he was just a kid.

"Mum's being a kid right now," I said. "Andy is a kid. I can't be the only grownup around here."

"I have to sleep," Jack said.

"Two hours," I said. "Then it's my turn."

He went down the ladder. I called after him, "Sleep under the table. It's better."

Two hours later he came up the ladder. His eyes were bloodshot and it was a bad hair day. But he came.

Andy was sitting on the floor next to me, carefully cleaning the oil off the baby crab with toilet paper. He liked sitting by my feet.

"The engine isn't going to work, is it?" I said to Jack.

"No." He ran his hands through his hair as if that would start his brain working.

"It would take us forever to sail back against the wind," I said.

"Mum wet the bed," Andy said.

Oh please no.

Andy sounded a bit satisfied. Like he was pleased to know it wasn't just little kids that wet the bed. He sounded scared too.

"Take the wheel," I said to Jack.

I went down and forward to Mum's little cabin. She was lying there in her sleeping bag, awake, just looking up at the ceiling. And Andy was right.

"Mum," I said. Then I lost it. "MUM!" I screamed.

It was like I wasn't there.

I did my breathing exercise for panic attacks that Arthur taught me. Then I talked quietly. In my calm, grownup way. "Mum, you can't wet the bed. You'll catch cold. We can't dry anything properly out here."

She just looked at the ceiling. I don't know where she was in her head.

"Mum, we'll get you home. We'll get all of us home. Just

fine. Jack's looking after us. He's steering right now. Andy's cleaning the baby crab. The whole crab family's fine."

Talk to me, Mum.

"Mum, I'll make you a deal. Every time I go on watch and every time I come off, I'll take you to the bathroom and then I'll take you back to bed. Every three hours. I'll do that, and you'll be good, and not make mistakes in between."

She didn't say anything.

"I'll take that for a yes," I said.

After I dragged Mum to the bathroom and cleaned up I went back up to Jack.

"I'm going to sleep," I said. "You turn us round so we can get back to the Canaries."

"It'll take weeks," Jack said.

"No, it won't. Turn us round."

"Mum's sick," Jack said.

"She's the zombie from hell."

"We take Mum back like this," Jack said, "and they'll put her in the snake pit."

Mum calls the hospital the snake pit.

"And they'll fry her brain," Jack said.

One time Dad came home from the hospital really angry. The big doctor wanted to give Mum electric shocks. Dad told the big doctor he'd kill him if he did. I'm surprised they didn't put Dad in a bed, he was that mad.

I watched this film on TV with Mum where Jack Nicholson was in the hospital. He wasn't really crazy, just pretending. Jack Nicholson told jokes and goofed around and stuff, and the people who ran the mental hospital didn't like it. So they fried his brain and he was a vegetable after that.

Afterward I asked Mum if they were ever going to fry her brain.

"Electric shocks, you mean?" she said.

"Yes."

"They say they work for some people," Mum said.

No, Mum, no, I thought.

"If you want to be one of the plastic people," she said.

I don't think Arthur could stop them from frying Mum's brain. Not if she was wetting her bed and had neglected her children when they were in danger on the sea.

So now when Jack said they'd put Mum back in the snake pit, I said, "How long will it take us to get to the West Indies?"

"Twenty-four to thirty days," Jack said. Like he knew.

"How do we know Mum will be better then?"

"She'll be better," Jack said. Like saying it could make it so.

"Can we call Dad on the radio and tell him what's happening?"

"The radio has a range of twenty miles," Jack said.

"Oh."

"Anyway, we can't tell anybody," he said.

And that's how we decided to keep going straight, all the way across the ocean.

Five

Jack

I can't work out where we are. Skip said to head 260, so we're heading 260. I can't do the math. I tried to shoot the sun with the sextant, like Skip taught me. I couldn't. Maybe I'm too tired. Maybe I'm too stupid. Andy told me not to cry.

When I was six my best friend Dave moved away. I waved his family away in their car. Then I ran home and banged into my mother in the hall. She just put her hands on my shoulders and pulled my face to her stomach. That's how tall I was. Her tummy was so warm. The tears all over my face made it hot too.

"You love Dave," Mum said over my head. "That's why you're crying."

She held me strongly. I cried some more for a while.

"Love is good," Mum said. "That's why you're hurting now."

Orrie

When Jack and Andy and me get ashore and the social workers find out about Mum, they'll probably send us all to a children's home. Then Dad will rescue us. That would be good.

Not if he's living with that Libby.

Libby's my age. OK, maybe a little older. But she has the mental age of Andy's crabs. I went to visit Dad in New York and she sat me down on the couch and gave me a big bowl of peanut butter pecan crunch ice cream. She told me she wanted us to rap and explore the little girl inside both of us. I really like peanut butter pecan crunch, so I didn't throw up in her face.

My dad's probably going to marry her.

Jack and me are tired, all the time, every minute. To keep the boat on course I have to wrestle with the wheel. It swings one way, and I'm already spinning the wheel madly the other way to bring it back on course. And then it swings back, and I'm swinging the wheel the other way. That takes strength. I'm not strong.

It takes strength to hang on to the cleat on the side and keep my feet braced against the front of the wheelhouse and my back braced against the raised seat behind me. I have to do that and tense all my muscles all the time, or I fall over. I fall over anyway.

When I sleep my muscles are tense so the boat won't throw me around.

My eyes are tired the whole time from looking out to sea.

I'm working twelve hours a day. I never sleep more than three hours. Andy always wakes me up in the middle of a dream.

All twelve hours I have to concentrate the whole time. If I slip up the boat would be sideways to the sea and the sails would flap and maybe we'd roll over. No mistakes. Twelve hours a day.

I'm too tired to cook. Candy bars make me sick. Andy opens cans of baked beans for me. At night I tie a box of corn flakes round my stomach with a rope and take handfuls from the box as I steer.

Jack

I'm tired all the time. There's always one of us sleeping under the table, me or Orrie. Sometimes Andy comes under the table with me and sleeps tucked under my arm.

Me and Orrie hardly see each other except when we're switching places at the wheel.

I made myself sit down at the chart table in the wheelhouse. I got out the chart of the Atlantic Ocean. I took a pencil and a ruler and drew a line from where we last knew we were to Antigua. I measured the line with a compass. It was 260. Thank God.

Even Charles Cresswell in my class probably couldn't do that.

Then I went out back and saw how many miles we'd done on the milometer that trails off the back. I marked off the miles on my line on the chart.

I told Orrie to keep steering 260. By my reckoning we've done five days and we have twenty-three to go.

I'm guessing.

Orrie

Jack says it's not good for Andy to do all the cooking. He's worried Andy's going to burn himself or something.

I told Jack if I have to be a hundred years old the whole time, there's no reason Andy can't be eleven and do all the cooking.

Some nights Andy makes baked beans and ketchup. The first time he burned the beans to the bottom of the pot and had to spend hours scrubbing.

I told Jack this is a little kid on a small boat. He needs to run around. He needs to do things. We have no television. The child must work.

Andy needs to feel useful. If he feels useful, he won't feel scared. He'll believe it when Jack says Mum's going to be fine.

Andy lights the stove all by himself and everything. He

gets up on the bunk beside the stove to stir and pour things in—he's too short to see over the edge of the stove.

Another night he made us Shredded Wheat with hot Spaghetti-Os poured over them. Last night we had canned ravioli with peanut butter and jelly sauce. Andy's not afraid to experiment.

Of course we never eat together like real people, because one of us always has to steer. So Andy cooks and Jack eats at the table and tells Andy how good it is. Then Jack takes the wheel and I sit at the table and tell Andy how good it is. He beams when you say that. Then Andy cleans our dishes and goes forward to feed Mum.

Dad's friend Libby has no fashion sense whatsoever.

Jack
We've done nine days and we have nineteen days to go.

When I steer I wander off course all the time. Orrie probably does too.

Who knows where we went when we were drifting.

Who knows what the current is doing to us.

Maybe the wind blows us sideways.

I worry about the crabs. I haven't said anything to Andy.

I did my project in school last year on crabs.

"Why do you want to do crabs?" my teacher Mrs. Lessing said.

"I just do," I said.

What I learned about crabs is they have no morals at all. If you put crabs together in a pot, they get hungry. And when they get hungry they eat each other. Put five crabs in a pot and come back two weeks later and what you have is one very big crab.

Andy has five crabs in a pot.

"Don't you think your crabs are a bit crowded in that pot together?" I said to him. We were lying under the table. I was trying to get to sleep but he was wriggling.

"No," Andy said. "They like each other. They're a family."

"What are you feeding them?" I said.

"Tuna fish."

"A lot?" I said. "Crabs need a lot to eat."

I started to go to sleep and he started wriggling again.

"We're out of tuna fish," Andy said.

"We had lots of cans," I said.

"Little cans," Andy said.

"What are you going to feed the crabs now?"

"Canned Mexican dinners."

Orrie and I tried to be polite when Andy made us canned Mexican dinners. But he must have noticed. I have nothing against Mexican food. I am sure Mexican people in Mexico do not eat canned Mexican dinners. "Crabs eat just about anything," I said.

"You didn't like it," Andy said. He sounded very small.

"No. I liked it. What I meant was I did my project on crabs, and I know if they're hungry they'll eat anything." I got an A plus on my project. Mrs. Lessing said it was the best crab project she'd ever seen.

"They'll eat canned Mexican dinners then," Andy said. "Together. They're a family. They like to eat together."

"Maybe they want some time to themselves as well," I said. "Maybe they need some privacy."

"What's privacy?" Andy said.

"Time to be alone. Maybe they could each have their own pot to sleep in and meet a couple of times a day to eat and play."

"They don't want that," Andy said.

"Yes they do. I know. I did my project on crabs. They're happiest when they have some time to themselves."

"They weren't by themselves back home in the Canary Islands," Andy said.

"But now they're in captivity," I said. I really wanted to go to sleep. But I kept seeing Andy taking the top off his pot and seeing only the daddy crab with just the baby's claw in its mouth. And I kept seeing me having to explain it to him. "They're pets," I said. "Pet crabs need time to themselves to cope with all the new stuff of being pets."

"You sure?" Andy said. He trusts me because I'm his big brother.

"I'm sure."

He went to sleep, just like that. I woke him up. "Promise me you'll put them all in separate pots?" I said.

"Yunh," he grunted sleepily.

I shook him. "Promise?"

"OK," he said, "promise." And then he went back to sleep.

I got up and put all the crabs in separate pots.

Orrie

This morning while I steered I watched Andy on deck. He was just sitting there, by the mainmast, not moving, still as could be.

At first I couldn't see why. Then I noticed. There was a little bird, about four feet off the deck, sitting on a rope between two stays. You couldn't see Andy watching the bird. But he was.

After forever, maybe an hour, Andy got up slowly. He took two paces forward and sat down near the bird. I kept taking my eyes off Andy—I had to steer all the time. I looked back and Andy was standing near the bird, his palm held out. There was nothing in his palm. He was still. The bird hopped onto his palm.

Fast, Andy moved his other hand over the palm and trapped the bird.

He unclipped his harness and brought it into the wheel-house to show me. He lifted his hand a bit. It was a little finch or something, with a chunky little beak and tan feathers and a downy white chest, hardly more than a baby.

Jack came up for his watch and looked at the bird over Andy's shoulder. "It's a land bird," he said. "A long way from home."

"He's tired," Andy said.

You could see the little bird's heart beating in his chest. "He's frightened," I said.

"He's flown hundreds of miles from land," Jack said.

"Really?" Andy said.

"That's why he's so tired," Jack said. "If he hadn't found the *Good Company* to rest on, he'd be dead."

"I saved his life?" Andy said.

"Yes," we both said.

Andy went below grinning and I gave Jack the wheel and followed him.

"Where's my crabs?" Andy screamed from below.

"I put them all in different pots," Jack shouted back.

I was trying to go to sleep under the table. Andy was looking for his other pots and holding the bird in one hand.

"Hey, Andy," Jack shouted from the wheel. "Don't put the bird in with a crab." He sounded really worried.

"How can I cook with no pots?" Andy yelled back.

"I'm trying to sleep," I shouted.

"Put the bird in the mosquito net," Jack shouted from the wheel house. There was a little mosquito net hanging above Jack's bunk.

"No," I screamed back. "The bird will beat his wings and break them." Men. "Don't do it, Andy," I said.

"What can I do?" Andy said.

"Put the bird forward in Mum's cabin," I said.

I went to sleep on the floor, bang.

A minute and a half later Andy shook me awake. He didn't have the bird in his hand any longer. "What about when we open Mum's door for you to take her to do her business?" Andy said. "The bird will fly out."

"We'll close the door from the wheelhouse to the deck first. Then if he gets out we can catch him again," I said, and went back to sleep.

Two minutes later Andy shook me awake again. "The bird's name is Travel-wavel," he said.

"Great," I said. "Thanks."

TRAVEL WAVEL
SITTING ON A ROPE

When I got up I opened the cabin door to take Mum to the head. That's what you call the bathroom at sea. "Shut the wheelhouse door," Andy said quietly from inside Mum's cabin.

"Sorry," I said. I closed the cabin door and went and closed the wheelhouse door. Then I went back to Mum's cabin.

Mum was lying down on her bunk in her sleeping bag like she always does. Travel-wavel was sitting on her head, on her hair. Andy had a bowl full of the God-knows-what gunk he cooks.

I stood in the door and watched. First Andy put a spoonful of gunk in Mum's mouth. She sort of helped him by closing her lips so the food got in her mouth.

Then Andy held a spoonful of gunk out to the little bird and it had a few pecks. Then he put the same spoon back in Mum's mouth.

Birds carry diseases. I guess that's another thing we aren't worrying about any more.

I just stood and watched. Andy was so careful in how he did it. So slow and gentle. He made no sound.

The bird was really hungry. You could tell.

Jack

By my calculations it's twelve days to go. I hope.

I like sailing at night. We never have to change the angle of the sails. The wind behind us always blows in the same direction. It's the trade winds. They're unbelievable. They took Columbus straight to the New World, and they're taking us.

I'm alone at night. Sometimes Andy's up too. He talks to

me and tells me stories about his animals. But I don't really have to listen. He's just talking. And mostly he's asleep.

I steer by a star. There's a big compass in front of the wheel, with a little green light in it that makes a soft glow that fills the wheelhouse. It's always the same course. I line the boat up so the needle on the compass points to 260. And then I pick a star, right by the edge of the mast, high up, a bright star. And I sail so I keep that star just the littlest bit to one side of the mast. I imagine the life forms who live on that star, see them looking down on us, sending radio messages we are not advanced enough to understand.

I think about getting to Antigua. There's a tropical beach there, with palm trees hanging over the water. As we pull into the dock Orrie's German friend Ilse is there. She's wearing her orange bikini because it's always summer in the West Indies. I let Orrie steer, even though it's hard to steer into land under sail, but she's learned a lot. I'm standing on the bowsprit with the landing rope in my hand. I have my shirt off and my chest is bronze from the sun. My hair is streaked white from the sun, like the guys on *Baywatch*. We almost touch the dock—Orrie has learned a lot—and I jump from the bowsprit to the land.

Ilse can't stop herself—she just runs forward and kisses me then and there. It's an impulse thing. She's just so excited. Everybody's watching. I kiss her right back.

She thinks I'm the most wonderful man in the world. She's wearing only her bikini bottom.

Orrie came up to take over the wheel. "That bird crapped in my hair," she said.

Andy came up right behind her saying, "No, it didn't."

"Andy forgot to close the cabin door and it went to sleep on my head," Orrie said.

"Travel-wavel's OK," Andy told me. "I opened a can of Spaghetti-Os and he came right to it."

"Good," I said.

"Now I've got bird crap in my hair," Orrie said. "I'm beyond filthy, venturing where no woman has gone before."

"It wasn't Travel-wavel's fault," Andy said.

"Why not?" Orrie said. "You held him over my head and squeezed him till the crap came out?"

"Don't hurt Travel-wavel," Andy said.

Orrie stopped and stood very still. "What do you think I am?" she asked Andy.

"Somebody take the wheel. I need some sleep," I said.

I pulled the sleeping bag over my head so nobody could crap in my hair.

Orrie

At noon Jack messed around at the chart table while I steered. Then he said there's only ten days to go to Antigua.

"Do you think the social workers will send us to the children's home when we get there?" I said.

"No," Jack said. "Dad will be there."

"He'll be in Antigua. We don't have a clue where we'll land," I said.

Jack took the wheel.

"We'll probably miss Antigua," I said. "Sail on into nothing."

"We'd hit South America," Jack said. That's how I knew—whatever he says, he doesn't know where we're going either.

"It's the children's home," I said.

"Get some sleep," Jack said.

"They'll lock Mum up."

"We won't tell them where Mum is," Jack said.

"Three kids sail into port and say we just sort of found this boat? Get real."

"We'll tell them to phone Dad in Antigua," Jack said.

"He'll probably have Mum committed to the hospital." I didn't know what I was saying until it came out of my mouth.

Jack didn't say anything back.

"Hospitals in poor countries have rats," I said.

Jack thought. He always thinks. Then he said: "Dad wouldn't do that."

"He left us." I didn't know I was going to say that either.

"He didn't leave us," Jack said. "He flies back every month to see us."

Mum says if Dad's making enough money selling his body in New York to fly back every month, he's making enough money to give her some more.

Dad's not really selling his body. He's really writing ads for a medical company. Mum just says he's selling his body because she's angry. I haven't told her about Libby. I don't think Jack has either.

I went to bed. Who knows what Dad will do?

I asked Arthur once if Mum had an illness. He said no. She was just very sad and very desperate.

"So why is she in a hospital?" I said.

"We say they're sick," Arthur said. "If we say people are desperate, everybody just gets frightened of them. But really she's just afraid and has lost hope."

"Oh," I said.

"If we say they're sick, people are nicer to them, and they think maybe we can cure them."

"Can't you cure them?" I said.

"They cure themselves," Arthur said. "When they can bear feeling their feelings again."

"Do they always cure themselves?"

Arthur looked me in the face, carefully, and said, "No." Then he watched my face to see how I'd react. He had bushy eyebrows.

"Do all nurses think like you?" I said.

"No," he said. "Lots of nurses and doctors think differently."

"Some of them think Mum's sick?" I said.

"Yes," he said.

"Why?" I asked.

"I think they can't bear looking at her," Arthur said.

People shouldn't say things like that to children.

A few minutes ago Andy came up to the wheelhouse in the dark and asked me if Mum was sick again.

"Yes," I said.

"Will she get better?"

"Of course," I said.

Jack

Six days to go, I think.

Orrie

Mum blocked up the toilet. I don't know how. She's not eating much. Maybe it's not her fault. The pipe's not very big. There was water and stuff leaking all over the floor into the main cabin. I had to clean the floor, and then I had to clear out the pipe. With my hand. Because I'm the girl. Pulling all the toilet stuff out with my hand, handful after handful. Down on my knees, cramped on the floor of the tiny bathroom. The smell.

I couldn't do it any more. The toilet was still blocked. I was crying. I stood up and went forward to Mum's cabin.

She was still in her sleeping bag. Zombie. Undead. Her head was turned away, her face to the wall. I screamed at her: "Mum. You're not a Mum. You're not fit to be a Mum. You're a crazy old lady. A dirty filthy old woman. You ought to be locked up. They're going to lock you up. They ought to fry your brain, you dirty old woman."

She didn't move, didn't turn.

"You don't care," I screamed. "You're stupid. You don't care."

Andy was tugging at my sweater. I looked down. He was looking up at me. His face was afraid. I felt terrible for screaming at Mum in front of him.

"Me clean toilet," Andy said.

"It's all right," I said. "People shout sometimes. It's over now."

"Me do it. Me little kid. Me like toilet stuff."

"It's OK, Andy," I said.

"Please," he said, so I let him.

I had to sleep in my bunk because the floor under the table was still too wet to lie on.

When I woke up Andy was cooking some gunk on the stove.

"I finished," he said proudly. "I did it all."

"Thank you, Andy," I said. I was still in my sleeping bag.

"Toilet works now," Andy said.

"Great, Andy. I'm really grateful," I said. "What are you cooking?"

"Don't know. There was a picture of a potato on the can. But there's brown stuff in it too." Andy can open cans all by himself, but he can't read. He's missing a lot of school. "I found some little cans with a fish on them for the crabs too," he said.

"Sardines," I said. "They'll like that. Is the brown stuff meat?"

"Don't know. Brown stuff."

"Have you washed your hands, Andy?" I said.

He pretended he was looking at the gunk he was cooking.

"Andy," I said.

He stirred the pot like mad.

"Andy," I said in my final warning voice.

He looked at me like he'd been caught and was desperately searching his brain for a lie that would work. He couldn't find one. He turned pink. His ears stuck out and his blue eyes were big.

I used my big voice, each word spaced out, the voice that frightens armies: "Go . . . Wash . . . Your . . . Hands."

He went.

I didn't eat my gunk that night. I'm a vegetarian.

Jack

I think we're about four hundred miles from Antigua. Or someplace. I try not to worry Orrie. Pretty soon maybe we should stop sailing at night somehow or maybe we'll run into something.

Mum isn't getting any better. Maybe we'll have to sail around the West Indies for a while until she gets better enough to take into land. I don't know if we have enough food for that.

Orrie

I took Mum to the bathroom and back again. Then I sat down plonk on the little bunk facing her and went to sleep sitting up. When I woke up I was lying flat, bouncing up and down every time the boat rolled.

Andy was sitting on Mum's bunk, talking to her, his legs crossed like Buddha. Travel-wavel was on Andy's head, holding on to his hair with little claws. Andy didn't mind. He was telling Mum a story. Her face was blank.

"There was this lady," Andy said. "She was the most beautiful lady in the world. She wanted to marry a beautiful prince. But her daddy wouldn't let her. Her daddy and mummy wouldn't let her marry anybody." Andy stopped and thought. "I don't know why," he said. "They were just bad. So the beautiful lady got mad with her whole family.

And she pricked her finger with a needle with poison on it and said that'll show them. All of them. And she died. But she wasn't really dead. She was really asleep forever. It was just like being dead. Except she was breathing and she didn't smell. Then the beautiful lady's mummy and daddy were very, very sorry. Too late! They put her on a special bed with special beautiful covers. She lay there for a hundred years and all her family died, one by one."

I knew why Andy was telling this story.

"One day a beautiful prince heard the story of the Sleeping Beauty. He liked looking at beautiful women. So he went to her house. But it was all covered with weeds, and flowers, and big trees, because her family were all old and dead and couldn't take care of it. The prince cut his way through with his shiny sword."

I was pretending to be asleep, but I looked at Andy. He was leaning over Mum's face.

"The prince looked at Sleeping Beauty for hours," Andy said. "And then he kissed her. She woke up, and they lived happily ever after."

He leaned down and kissed Mum on the forehead, hard. Her face didn't change, not one little bit. But her whole body shook.

Andy waited while she shook. Gradually she stopped moving. Her face was still blank. Andy saw I was watching.

He looked ashamed, and beaten. He got down off Mum's bunk and went into the main cabin. Travel-wavel was still hanging onto his hair.

Jack

The weather changed on my midnight watch. The wind has gone down and seems to be moving around. The sails flap a lot. Most of the stars are gone, so it must be cloudy. Something's wrong. And the waves feel different—longer somehow.

When I handed over to Orrie at three I told her to wake me up if it gets any worse.

Six

Orrie

Jack's such a worrywart. Telling me to wake him up like he's in charge.

The sail's flapping a lot.

I like it at night. I can think.

I think I'm going to be a nurse when I grow up. Or a doctor. I can't decide. Doctors have more power. They can decide whether to cut a baby open, or fry somebody's brain, or anything. You can really make a difference if you're a doctor.

But nurses are nicer. That's my experience. Nurses can really talk to sick people. Doctors make much more money.

But money is not everything in a person's life. If you're a doctor you can't be a caseworker.

I won't be a gooey nurse, saying how are we today. I'll be a serious nurse. My patients will do exercises every morning so they don't lie in bed and get depressed.

Maybe I'll win an award for being such a good nurse. I really want to help people. I can see myself at some Academy Awards for nurses. I'm standing up in the front, holding the Oscary thing in my hands. My eyes are all watery. All my grateful patients who nominated me for the award are in the audience cheering and clapping. I'm saying how I'm thanking everybody.

And Mum's there too, and she's happy, so happy for me. And Dad's there too. He brought Libby, and she's old and fat now. She's dyed her hair red to conceal where she's going bald, and the hair dye's run, and it's running down her cheeks and staining her face.

Dad wishes he was back with us.

Jack

I couldn't sleep because the boat was moving funny. I didn't want to think about it. I lay in my sleeping bag and thought about Antigua.

I asked Ilse if she wanted to go for a walk. She said yes. The palm trees were hanging over the water in the moonlight. I put my arm around her as we walked along the beach. She didn't seem to mind. We were barefoot and the sand was cool between our toes. We stopped and turned our faces to each other. "Jack," Orrie shouted. "Get up here."

Orrie

I'd been watching us get closer and closer to the ship. It was an oil tanker or a big freighter or something. The moon was hidden behind it. The ship looked like a great black mountain on the sea, with the moonlight outlining the edges. I could see a red light in the middle and a white light on the bow. Our course looked like we were going straight at it. I wasn't sure what the sails would do if I changed course. I called Jack.

He came right up. So did Andy.

Jack stared. "She looks beautiful," he said.

The roll of the wave would take us up so we saw the whole ship. Then we'd go down and for a moment we'd lose sight of it.

"Are we going to hit it?" I asked Jack.

"I don't know. She's so beautiful."

"I can't see," Andy said.

Jack held him up on the chart table so he could see out the window of the wheelhouse. Andy's eyes went wide. "I'll tell Mum," he said. Jack put him down. "Ship," Andy shouted as he went down the ladder. "Ship, Mum, ship."

Jack went and took the handset from the radio on the wall over the chart table. The radio crackled. "I think it's the right band," Jack said. Skip must have shown him how to use it when I was sick.

"Hullo," Jack said into the handset. "*Good Company* calling freighter. Hullo. *Good Company* calling freighter. Over."

"*African Pride*," a deep man's voice said. "*African Pride* calling *Good Company*. You're not on my radar. Where are you? Over."

"Close. We're too small to show up on radar," Jack said. How did he know that? "Where are you headed? Over."

"Out of Lagos, running for New York," the man said.

It was strange, talking to a man high on that ship in the dark. We hadn't seen anybody in almost a month. The ocean is a big and empty place.

"My name's Oliver," the man said. "What's yours, *Good Company*? Over."

"Jack. Over."

I was thinking: This man could save us. I knew Jack was thinking it too.

Jack

I was thinking: How do I ask him where we are?

"I thought you were a woman, Jack," Oliver on the *African Pride* said. "You got a high voice on this set. Over."

"I am. A woman called Jack." I didn't want him to know we were kids. "My husband's asleep and I'm on watch. Over."

"You a yacht, *Good Company*? Over," Oliver said. I could see the lights on his bridge, riding high above us, maybe three miles away. His voice was in my ear.

"Yes," I said. If I asked him where we were, he'd know something was wrong. But I could tell him where we were going, and then if I was wrong, maybe he'd say something. "We're out of the Canaries, running for Antigua. Over," I said.

"You ready for the storm, Jack? Over," Oliver said.

"Storm?"

He said nothing.

"Over," I said.

"There's a storm coming," Oliver said. "Force Ten. Aren't you listening to your radio? Over."

"Force Ten," I said. I didn't know what Force Ten was.

"Bad?" Orrie hissed at me.

I nodded. I could tell that from Oliver's voice.

There was Mum's face. She was at the bottom of the ladder looking up at me. I could just see her head and shoulders in the little moonlight that got down there. Andy must have got her up.

"He can rescue us," Orrie said to Mum.

"Yes," I said.

"Hey, *Good Company*. Hey, Jack. Over," the radio said.

"The storm's going to be very bad," Orrie said to Mum.

Mum's eyes were on me. I made a mistake. I looked right into her eyes. There was nothing there. Holes.

If they took us now she'd lose custody of us forever and her life would be over.

I looked at Orrie. She was staring at Mum too.

"Orrie," I said quietly.

"Yes," she said.

We both knew there was no choice.

"We're as ready for a storm as we'll ever be," I said into the handset. "I'm going to wake my husband up now and batten down the hatches."

I didn't want to stop talking to Oliver. He was a good person, a good man in the emptiness. It sounded warm on his ship. But if I kept talking he'd figure out about us. "Over and out," I said.

"Good luck, *Good Company*. Over and out," *African Pride* said, and we were alone on the ocean.

"What's Force Ten?" Orrie said.

"I don't know," I said.

I gave Orrie the wheel and put my safety harness on. I went out and took the smaller sails down, the mizzen in the stern and the jib in front. I didn't think we'd be needing them. The wind was rising. I was slipping and sliding on the deck.

Orrie

Jack was taking down the sails. I was at the wheel. Andy was standing on the ladder, trying to get Mum to come up into the wheelhouse.

"It's magic," he said to Mum. "Like fairyland. All lights."

Mum didn't say anything. I couldn't see her face from where I stood. I could only see the back of Andy's head.

"Magic," Andy said. Somehow his voice was calm, with no worry in it. He just wanted her to feel the magic. He's not afraid of madness. He grew up with it.

Mum followed Andy up the ladder. At the top she was all floppy. I thought she might fall over.

"It's there," Andy said. He pointed to the front window of the wheelhouse. Mum turned her body round and looked.

Andy was too small to see out the window. He stood between us, holding Mum's hand. I looked at the ship with Mum. I had to, or we'd run into it.

Mum braced herself against the front of the wheelhouse, her eyes up against the glass. Andy couldn't see out. I couldn't lift him. I was steering. He didn't ask Mum to lift him. I looked at him. His whole face was happy.

Mum was crying. No sounds. I didn't know what she was feeling.

I kept trying to wrestle the wheel.

"Oliver's my friend," Andy said to Mum. "He's in that ship."

Jack pulled the outside door shut with a bang. He stared at Mum.

"Start the engine," I said. "We're going to need it."

"I can't," Jack said. "It's full of spaghetti."

"It's full of what?" I said.

Jack

"Spaghetti-Os," I said to Orrie. "Skip poured a can of Spaghetti-Os into the fuel so the engine wouldn't work."

Mum turned and looked at me because I'd said Skip's name.

"Why?" Orrie said.

I looked at Orrie not Mum. "He said it was because of women. Said no woman could make him use the engine." I could feel Mum breaking without looking at her. I hated her.

"Oh, Mum," Orrie said.

Mum was sitting on the floor of the wheelhouse.

"Who cares any more?" I said. I went to the ladder and Mum scooted out of my way.

I went down the ladder and got the how-to-sail book. There wasn't enough light in the cabin to read. I didn't dare turn on a light any more. They're going dim. I think the battery's running out because we don't use the engine. So I took the book back up to the wheelhouse.

The wheelhouse was full of moonlight. Mum was sitting in the front corner, on the other side from the wheel. She had her feet stuck out in front of her, and Andy was lying in her lap sucking his thumb. I pretended she wasn't there.

I sat in the back corner at the chart table. I flipped madly through the book. I couldn't see the pages. I was too nervous. I made myself slow down and breathe. The boat was moving funny, like the waves were suddenly getting bigger.

Orrie

Good Company rose and fell on the waves from the *African Pride*. We passed right under the freighter's stern, about four hundred yards away, and the water was boiling with the backwash from her engines.

Jack was scared, but I was laughing at the wheel. I love cutting things close. The ship was high above us, like a great black city. Jack was holding Andy up so he could see. And then we were past.

The sky was changing on my left. It must have been dawn, but we couldn't see the sun. The sky looked dirty now, and the waves were gray and flat and long.

"What's Force Ten?" I said to Jack. He was reading the how-to-sail book.

"A storm," he said.

"A big storm?"

"Yes."

Jack

The how-to-sail book said to put out a "sea anchor" and showed you how. So I took the bucket full of rope we keep in the cockpit in case anybody falls overboard. I made sure the bucket was tied to the end of the rope and threw it overboard.

The rope spun out behind us. That was a funny feeling. Then the rope reached the end and the bucket filled with water. You could feel the bucket sort of jerk the boat. The book said the drag would keep us straight and slow us down.

Orrie

It was past Jack's turn to steer. Two hours past. I didn't say anything. I was really tired. But he was doing stuff on deck to get ready for the storm.

The waves are different now. Bigger. My stomach feels funny. I hope it's not seasickness. I hope it's just fear.

Jack

The book says to reef the mainsail. It has a picture showing you how. There are these little strings in a row halfway down the sail and you tie them down around the wooden boom at the bottom of the sail. Then only a bit of the sail is left for the wind to push.

But first you have to get the sail down.

Orrie

Jack didn't tell me. He just let the mainsail down. It was the only sail we had up. It came crashing down, flopping and plopping all over the place. Jack couldn't get to it. His safety harness was holding him back. I saw him unclip his harness so he could move. I screamed at him but he couldn't hear me.

How could I steer without a sail?

We still had momentum. We were still going straight. I prayed. We climbed to the top of a wave. When you get to the top, each time, the rudder comes out of the water and the wheel goes slack in your hands. It did it again. The boat started to turn sideways into the wind.

We started down the wave. The waves were bigger. The wind was bigger. The storm was coming. As we went down the wave the rudder bit into the water. The wheel went wild in my hands. I couldn't stop it. We turned sideways to the wave, falling down it.

Out the window I saw Jack falling across the deck, holding onto the boom and the sail.

Jack

I was on deck when we turned sideways to the wave. The boat leaned over and everything fell to the low side. I could see the wave above me, gray and green and high. I was grabbing at the sail, pulling it in. I had to feel for the little rope ties under the sail, and then pull them under the boom and tie them together on the other side. I don't know knots. I just did whatever.

The sail kept blowing out of my hands in the wind. As we rolled up each wave the sail and everything fell to the down side, dragging me with it. My knees got scraped. I was bruised. I had to hold on. On and on. Thrown from side to side.

I'd done it. The sail was tied down. Now we needed the reduced sail back up so we could steer. I went to the mast to haul on the rope to raise the sail. I clipped my harness back on to a safety rope. I couldn't raise the sail. It was too hard to pull. The force of the wind was too much. I used the winch. That made it easier. But the winch handle kept slipping out. I was swearing all the time.

The sail was partway up. At the top of the wave the wind filled the sail and the wooden boom came whipping across the boat. I leapt out of the way in front of the mast. I stood there and kept turning the winch. It kept slipping. The boom was crashing back and forth, the ship rolling.

I did it. The sail was up.

I got down on my hands and knees and crawled aft back to the cockpit, keeping low so the boom wouldn't knock me overboard as it came across.

Orrie

I love my brother.

Jack came back in all wet. He grabbed the wheel and stood

next to me. As we came to the top of the wave the rudder came out of the water and the wheel went slack. Jack turned so he was at a corner to me and pulled on the spokes of the wheel with all his weight. I turned the wheel like crazy too. That turned the rudder, still sitting out of the water.

A second after we started down the wave the rudder bit into the water. The pressure on the wheel was enormous. I threw myself over next to Jack and we held onto the wheel with both our weights and the boat turned. I was already over to the other side of the wheel, and Jack was with me. We pulled it back the other way so fast the boat didn't swing too far.

Now we were going straight before the wind again. We were all right. We fell to the bottom of one wave and climbed to the top of the next one. Mum was watching us from the corner.

"Is that Force Ten?" I said to Jack.

"No," he said.

Jack took the wheel. I went to be down in the main cabin, under the table. At noon I took the wheel again. More wind. Jack went downstairs and read the book. Then he came back up and tied the boom of the sail back so it can't swing across.

We can't take the sail down or we won't be able to steer. Jack says now the sail won't blow across and tear. But if I get too far off course the wind will get behind the sail and blow us over.

Jack went to bed.

At three Jack took the wheel and I went to sleep under the table.

Even there the boat was throwing me around. We would slide down the wave, the bow out of the water. Then we'd hit the bottom between the waves with a smash, and the force would bounce me off the floor. I knew I had to sleep. I was going to need all my strength. I didn't sleep. The noises of the sea and the water banging against the side of the boat were huge in the cabin. Maybe I'd feel safer up top.

When I stuck my head up the ladder Andy said: "Mum has to pee." He was in the corner of the wheelhouse with Mum.

"How do you know?" I said. Maybe she was talking.

"I know," Andy said.

I looked at Mum. She looked back at me like she needed to pee but wouldn't ask.

I was tired. "Just do it yourself," I said to Mum. "Go wet yourself."

Mum got up and looked around, confused, and ran toward the back door of the wheelhouse. I couldn't get to her. Jack screamed, a terrible unearthly shriek. Mum froze against the back door. Jack left the wheel and grabbed Mum. I lunged for the wheel. I had it, but with my back to the bow. There was no time to get across to the other side of the wheel. I steered looking out the back window, thinking backward.

Jack was pulling Mum across the wheelhouse. "I'll take her," he said to me.

He led her down the steps of the ladder. I got back behind the wheel the right way.

"Do I have to take her trousers off?" Jack yelled up from the cabin.

"No, she does that," I yelled back.

Jack

I got Mum into the bathroom and shut her in there and braced myself against the door so I wouldn't fall over.

Maybe I was supposed to be in there with her. I don't know. It's very strange for a boy, taking your mother to the bathroom.

When I hadn't heard anything for a few minutes I opened the door. Mum was sitting on the toilet lid, dressed, facing away from me. Her hair was all stringy and matted.

"I'm sorry," she said, without looking at me.

"It's OK, Mum," I said.

She stood up by herself. When she came out of the bathroom I was expecting her to go to her cabin. But she went back through the cabin and up the ladder into the wheelhouse. She sat in her corner, hugging her knees and shivering. I got a sleeping bag from her bunk and wrapped it round her. I guessed she was afraid and wanted to be with us.

"Jack," Orrie said.

I remembered it was still my watch. I took the wheel and Orrie went below to sleep.

Orrie

At six I took the wheel from Jack. The tops of the great waves around us were all breaking in white foam. "Is this Force Ten?" I said.

Jack's face was drawn. He looked sick. "I don't know," he said.

The wind grew. We flew. With that one little reduced sail, a little patch, we went faster, far faster than we had ever gone before.

The boat rode down the waves like a snowboard. It veered to one side and I pulled on it. Back and forth, like I'd been doing for weeks, but now it was harder to hold.

The full moon was out, dead in front, low in the sky. There was a road of shining white water and we were racing down it, racing toward the moon. The rest of the sea was black, sheer black in the moonlight. But everywhere the tops of the waves broke in rollers turned shining white by the light. And I tried to keep the boat going down the shining white road, zigging and zagging across it.

It was the most beautiful thing I have ever seen. I couldn't feel the beauty, because I was in terror.

And then I knew it was too hard, and I was too tired, and I couldn't hold it any longer. I yelled for Jack.

Jack

I took one look, grabbed the wheel next to Orrie, and we held on together.

"Thanks," Orrie said. "I can't do it alone."

"I can't either," I said.

And we stood next to each other, pulling together, and we moved as one.

But I knew we couldn't last forever, hour after hour after hour. The waves were breaking all around us now. Behind us a great wave broke on the cockpit with a screaming explosion. The stern of the boat went down and the bow went up so we couldn't see anything forward. We wrestled with the wheel and guessed how to point it.

We guessed right. The stern of the boat rose, the water cascading off it, I hoped, but I didn't dare look round.

I thought: The next big wave will hit the wheelhouse windows and break the glass and we will fill with water.

"Force Ten?" Orrie said.

"Yes," I said.

"My crabs." Andy's face was in the opening at the top of the ladder. He was crying. "My crabs are gone. Find my crabs."

"Forget the crabs," Orrie shouted.

Andy couldn't go looking round the boat. He'd be thrown around and cracked to bits.

"They could die," Andy wailed.

"You could die," Orrie screamed back.

I looked at Andy's face for a split second and then looked back at the racing sea. But I'd seen the awful quiet fear on his face.

"Be afraid," Orrie shouted at him. "Be very afraid."

I didn't look at Andy. I couldn't spare a second. Orrie moved with me. She had to be looking at the sea too.

"Go hold onto Mum," Orrie shouted at Andy. "Hold Mum's hand."

Next time I grabbed a look Andy was on Mum's lap, sucking his thumb, his eyes wide.

Orrie

I knew the storm would last all night. I knew I wouldn't. I knew that when I had to stop and let go of the wheel, Jack wouldn't be able to hold it alone. I hung on.

Then the boat jerked to one side and I lost my feet and it threw me across the wheelhouse. I slammed into the floor. For just a second there was nothing, and then bad pain in my ribs.

I made myself stand up because Jack couldn't do it alone. I slammed across the wheelhouse and pulled on the spokes with Jack. The pain in my ribs was unbelievable.

"I can't." I was crying. "I love you," I said to Jack. "I can't." Something was wrong in my chest.

I let go of the wheel. A roll threw me across the wheelhouse. I landed next to Mum and Andy. I was lying down. Mum was staring at me. I scrambled to my knees and grabbed her head in my hands. I put my face right up to hers so we were inches apart and I was looking right into her eyes. I held her head hard so she couldn't turn away. My ribs were screaming. I never want to see again what I saw in her eyes.

I spoke loudly so she could hear me in there: "We're your children. We're going to die. We need your help."

There was something in there. My hands were almost crushing her head. She was shaking.

Andy was standing. He bent over and kissed Mum on the forehead. She was shaking. Andy kissed her frantically, hard, on the forehead, the cheeks, the mouth, a little boy in terror. "Kiss," he said to me. "Kiss. Kiss her awake."

She was shaking. I let go of her head. I was crying because I couldn't look. Andy was kissing her. The boat was yawing every way. Mum was hitting at Andy's face, slapping him away, stopping him.

Andy stood there, beyond understanding, beyond crying. His face was a hundred years old.

Mum began to make a sound. A moaning, a crazy humming. She was still shaking. She was looking at Andy. She stood up, still moaning, slapping at her face and chest with her hands. "I'm sorry," she said to Andy.

"Help, Mum, help," Jack screamed.

Mum threw herself across the wheelhouse at Jack.

Jack

Mum threw herself across the wheelhouse at me and landed with her hands on the spokes of the wheel. She grabbed them to stand up. She was making a noise like an animal in a trap.

"No, Mum, no," I screamed, screeched, begging, trying to make my voice louder than the sound she was making. She was pulling the wheel away from me, turning us into the wave. I let go of the wheel, grabbed her with both hands and threw her to the other side of the wheel. She grabbed it and pulled again. We turned back. "Yes, Mum, yes," I shouted, and then we were going to turn into the wave the other side. I threw myself where she had been at first, yelling, "Push, don't pull. Push. Push," and she did. "Yes," I screamed, and she smiled across the wheel at me, like sunrise.

Orrie

"It's magic," Andy said to me.

"It's not magic," I said. Jack was still yelling at Mum, trying to make her do it right.

"We're going to die," Andy said to me happily. "But we're going to die like a family."

I fell asleep.

Jack

Mum was terribly floppy. Like the bits of her body didn't go together. Like she wanted to help me steer, but she'd forgotten how to move her arms and legs right.

I knew I couldn't last another minute. I knew I had to. "Stand next to me," I shouted. I was screaming from fear. She wasn't making those sounds any more. She stood next to me. "Move with me," I said. "Now," and I leaned to the left with all my weight, and she put her weight that way too. "Back," I screamed, and pushed back. For a second we were pushing against each other, and then she was with me again.

I kept my eyes on the sea ahead, not on Mum. I yelled orders and we moved together. My shoulders hurt bad.

"I'm sorry, Jack," Mum said beside me.

"It's OK," I said. I didn't look at her.

"I'm bad," she said.

I didn't say anything.

"I didn't look after my children," she said in a flat calm voice.

"Steer, Mum. Just steer."

She did. "Watch the water," I said. "So you can do it yourself."

She watched the water. After a very long time she said, "I think I can hold it myself if you want to sleep."

"Are you sure?"

"No," Mum said.

After another few minutes I said, "Mum, I have to lie down. Can you do it?"

"Yes," she said.

"I'm sorry, Mum," I said. "I can't. Will you be all right?"

"Maybe," Mum said.

I lay down on the wheelhouse floor.

Andy shook me awake. It was dawn. Mum was standing above me steering.

"It's all right," Andy said to me. "I found the crabs."

Seven

Orrie

When I woke up my chest still hurt. Mum said I must have bruised a rib. Mum and Jack took turns steering. The wind went down in the morning, but the waves were still big and long. In the afternoon the sun came out and the sky was full of fluffy clouds. We were back in the trade winds.

Mum and me went out to the back cockpit. We took off all our clothes, just leaving our harnesses on, and threw buckets of water over each other to get clean.

Mum looked too thin. I had forgotten she was beautiful. We dried ourselves in the sun.

"My hair's gone all stringy and split endy," Mum said.

I pulled some of my own hair over toward my eye so I could look at it. Yuck. "Mine too," I said.

"Mine's a lot worse than yours," Mum said.

"No it's not." I went and stood next to her and held some of my hair against hers. "See?"

We stood there naked in the sun, mother and daughter, talking bad hair.

"Are you all right, Mum?" I asked.

"No. But I'm better."

I let out my breath. Mum looked at me and laughed. "Nobody's really all right," Mum said, and we laughed and laughed.

Jack said we were getting pretty close to Antigua. Then we saw this yacht in the middle of the ocean. It looked bigger than us, and ever so much cleaner. But I love *Good Company*. Jack spoke to them on the radio. The boat was called the *Jolly Roger*, and the people were Juliet and Frank. They were out of Miami.

"Ask them where Antigua is," Mum said to Jack.

"I know where Antigua is," Jack said.

"Yes, but ask where we are," Mum said.

"I know where we are."

"Just ask them, OK?" Mum said.

"Who's that talking there, Jack? Over," Juliet said. She sounded old, like a grandmother.

"That's just my mother. She doesn't know anything," Jack said.

"Gimme that," Mum said, and grasped the handset.

It turned out we were two hundred miles south of Antigua and about to miss it and sail on into nowhere.

"I knew that," Jack said.

"Only two hundred miles off after crossing a whole ocean is really very good," Mum said.

"Mum," Jack shrieked.

Some people just can't take criticism. But it's good Jack can get angry with Mum now.

Jack

Why do I have to do everything around here? If they're so smart, why can't they do the navigation? Nobody ever says thank you. Orrie's taking Mum's side as usual.

Orrie

While Jack was down in the cabin sulking, Mum turned *Good Company* north and I set the sails for the new course. Jack came up and sat at the chart table and drew some new lines. Then he showed us how he'd been right all along. He said it would take two days to get to Antigua. But we better not sail at night, in case we ran into the island of Martinique, which is in the way.

"We could put into Martinique first," Mum said.

"No," I said. "Antigua."

Dad promised he'd be on the dock in Antigua.

Mum and I were sitting in the cockpit again. Jack was steering. He was OK now that he was back in charge.

Mum's face went empty again.

"Earth to Mum," I said.

Blank.

"Earth to Mum," I shouted.

She startled. "Sorry."

"What is it?"

"When we get to Antigua I have to call Skip's family," Mum said.

Skip has two sons, little kids. I met them once. They're younger than me. We all went to the zoo in London. I didn't like seeing all the animals in prison. Skip's boys had a great time.

"Do you want me to call them?" I said.

"No," Mum said. "I'll do it."

So she's better. But I'll be standing right next to her when she makes that call.

We saw Antigua. There was a big cliff at the end of the island, and we couldn't see a way into the harbor. But there was a boat ahead of us, a big ketch with white sails on the sparkling water. The ketch sailed straight for the cliff and we followed it.

It turned in front of us and seemed to sail into the cliff. I went outside with Andy to stand in the bow and yell if I saw any rocks underwater. Travel-wavel was sitting in Andy's hair.

We came to the cliff and I could see it was split in two and there was a passage between, on the right. We sailed through, the yellow cliffs high on either side, and the smell of land all around us.

We were through and the wind dropped. There was a long white beach on the right, with palm trees. Stuff so green it hurt your eyes went up from the beach to a hill far above. The water was light blue, and ahead of us there were houses and a narrow channel.

Travel-wavel let loose of Andy's hair and flew off toward the land.

"Travel," Andy screamed.

"He's found a home," I said. "Land is his home. You saved him. Now he's safe. See—he's waving goodbye with his wings."

Andy looked, and saw, and we both waved back to Travel-wavel until he was out of sight high on the hill.

Jack

I saw Orrie and Andy on the bow waving goodbye to Travel-wavel. I waved goodbye too. He's been a good bird.

I gave Mum the wheel and went down to check the crabs. They're still OK.

Orrie

I went back to the wheelhouse. We were coming to the narrow channel by the houses. Jack wanted me to sail the boat into the dock.

"No way," I said. "I'll ram the dock and smash the boat to pieces."

"Mum?" Jack said.

"Don't look at me," Mum said. "I'm the loony."

So Jack gave me the wheel and went forward to the bow to stand by the anchor rope. He took his T-shirt off in case any girls were looking. He thinks I don't know, but I do.

I looked over at the dock for Dad but couldn't see him. Behind the dock there were dark trees with red flowers. I couldn't look for long. The channel was narrow and I had to watch out. I turned *Good Company* into the wind like I'd seen other people do in the Canary Islands, and we came to a stop just right. Jack threw the anchor overboard. The rope ran out, and we anchored about two hundred feet from the dock.

That was it. I went out on deck and Jack and me shook hands.

Andy and Mum helped us take down the sails. I had my face in the mainsail when I heard my Dad whistle. When Dad whistles he sticks both his fingers in his mouth and it's really loud. I dropped the sail and turned round. Dad was on the dock, across the water.

I jumped overboard and started paddling for the dock, splashing fast. Jack was right behind me. Who cares about the sails. Dad tore off his shirt and was pulling his shoes off so he could jump in to meet us. I looked back. For a moment Mum and Andy were standing hand in hand on the edge of *Good Company*, and then they jumped into the water after us.